COCOA BEACH LIBRARY
3 2480 00053 7270

P9-CCZ-014

Keiko Kasza

Grandpa Toad's SECRETS

G.P. Putnam's Sons · New York

To Kimihiro and Rika

A special thanks to my husband, Greg,
who always reads my manuscripts
with the eyes of a scholar and the heart of a child

G. P. Putnam's Sons, a division of The Putnam & Grosset Group,
200 Madison Avenue, New York, NY 10016.
G. P. Putnam's Sons, Reg. U.S. Pat. & Tm. Off.
Published simultaneously in Canada.
Printed in Hong Kong by South China Printing Co. (1988) Ltd.
Text set in Kennerley O.S. Book designed by Sue H. Ng.

Library of Congress Cataloging-in-Publication Data
Kasza, Keiko. Grandpa Toad's secrets / Keiko Kasza. p. cm.
Summary: Grandpa Toad teaches his grandson the secrets of
survival, but Little Toad is the one who saves the day when
a huge monster attacks them.
[1. Grandfathers—Fiction. 2. Toads—Fiction. 3. Conduct of life.] I. Title.
PZ7.K15645Gr 1995 [E]—dc20 93-44376 CIP AC
ISBN 0-399-22610-9
1 3 5 7 9 10 8 6 4 2
First impression

One day Grandpa Toad and
Little Toad took a walk in the forest.

"You know, Little Toad," said Grandpa, "our world is full of hungry enemies."

"How can we protect ourselves, Grandpa?" asked Little Toad.

"Well," Grandpa declared, "I'm going to share my secrets with you. My first secret is to be brave. You must be brave when facing a dangerous enemy."

Just then a hungry snake appeared. "Hello, toads," hissed the snake. "I'm going to eat you for lunch!"

Little Toad screamed and ran away to hide. But was Grandpa scared?

Not a bit! "Eat me if you can!" Grandpa shouted fiercely. "But I may be more than you can swallow!"

Grandpa sucked in the air and got bigger and bigger.

"Well," murmured the snake, "maybe some other time." And the snake slithered away.

Little Toad jumped from the bushes. "Oh, Grandpa!" he cried. "You were so brave. You were wonderful!"

Grandpa Toad beamed with pleasure. "Thank you," he said. "But some enemies are too big to scare away. My second secret is to be smart. You must be smart when facing a dangerous enemy."

Just then a hungry snapping turtle appeared. "Hello, toads," snapped the snapper. "I'm going to snap you up for a snack. Snap! Snap!"

Little Toad screamed and ran away to hide. But was Grandpa scared?

Not a bit! "A snack?" asked Grandpa. "Wouldn't you rather have a feast?"

"Why, sure," said the snapper.

"Well," Grandpa whispered, "a tasty-looking snake slithered by just moments ago. If you hurry, you can catch him."

"Gee, thanks for the tip," said the turtle. And he hurried off to hunt the snake.

Little Toad jumped from the bushes. "Oh, Grandpa!" he cried. "You were so smart. You were wonderful!"

Grandpa Toad beamed with pleasure. "Thank you," he said. "Now, for my third and last secret." But before he could say another word…

A humongous monster appeared. “Hi, toads,” bellowed the monster. “I’m going to eat you guys just for the fun of it!”

Little Toad screamed and ran away to hide. But was Grandpa scared?

Yes, he was! He had never seen such a frightening creature in his life. He tried to run away but the monster caught him.

Little Toad hid in the bushes, shaking with fear. But he remembered his grandpa's secrets:

Be brave and be smart!

Be brave and be smart!

He saw some wild berries and quickly decided what to do.

Little Toad threw the berries at the monster. They splatted and left red spots all over his legs. The monster didn't even notice. He was too busy making Grandpa into a toad sandwich!

Little Toad stepped bravely out of the bushes. "Grandpa," he yelled, "let that poor monster go!"

"What?" said the monster.

"What?" yelled Grandpa.

"Grandpa," said Little Toad, "it's not very nice of you to go around poisoning monsters. Your poison is already creeping up his legs. Soon he'll have spots all over his behind. And then he'll die. Shame on you, Grandpa!"

The monster looked at his legs and shouted, "Help! Help! These mean toads are poisoning me!"

The monster ran away as fast as he could. Grandpa and Little Toad hugged each other.

"Whew!" sighed Grandpa. "That was a close call."

"It sure was," said Little Toad.

"Well," said Grandpa finally, "you still haven't heard my third secret."

"What's that?" asked Little Toad.

"My third secret is this," Grandpa declared. "In case of emergency, be sure to have a friend you can count on. Little Toad, you were brave. You were smart. You were wonderful!"

Now it was Little Toad who beamed with pleasure.